THAT FRUIT IS MINE!

ANUSKA ALLEPUZ

WALKER BOOKS
AND SUBSIDIARIES
LONDON · BOSTON · SYDNEY · AUCKLAND

Deep in the heart of the jungle,
lived five elephants.

In that jungle grew lots of fruit.
The elephants LOVED fruit.

Elephant One
munched on mangoes.

Elephant Two
craved coconuts.

Elephant Three
was keen on kiwis.

Elephant Four
banqueted on bananas.

And **Elephant Five**
preferred pineapples.

But one day, deep, *deep* in the heart
of the jungle, the elephants discovered
a new tree. A new, very TALL tree.

And on that very tall tree was the MOST delicious-looking exotic fruit that the elephants had ever seen.

EVERYONE wanted to eat it.

Hey, look at THAT!

"MINE!"

cried Elephant One.
"That fruit is MINE!"

She KNEW that she could reach it.
She *huffed* and she *puffed*
with all her might...

One,
two,
three,
four,
five.
Up,
up,
up!

PFFFT!

The fruit didn't move an itty bitty inch.

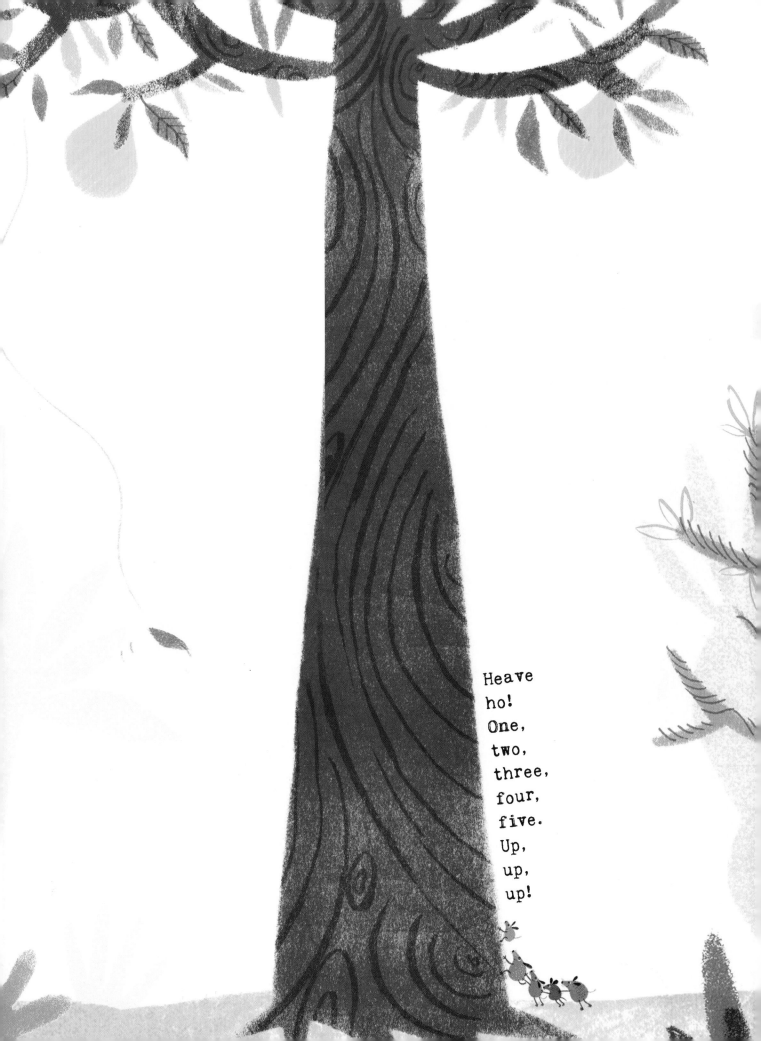

Heave
ho!
One,
two,
three,
four,
five.
Up,
up,
up!

"MINE!"
said Elephant Two.
"That fruit is MINE!"

She KNEW that she had a very smart idea. She could already taste that sweet, sweet fruit...

Keep stretching!

Look! A humongous bug!

Hmmm, perhaps her idea
needed a little more work.

"MINE!"

shouted Elephant Three.

"That fruit is MINE!"

He KNEW that he was cleverer

than Elephant One and Elephant Two.

So, with a he-e-e-eave

and a stre-e-e-etch,

he started to climb...

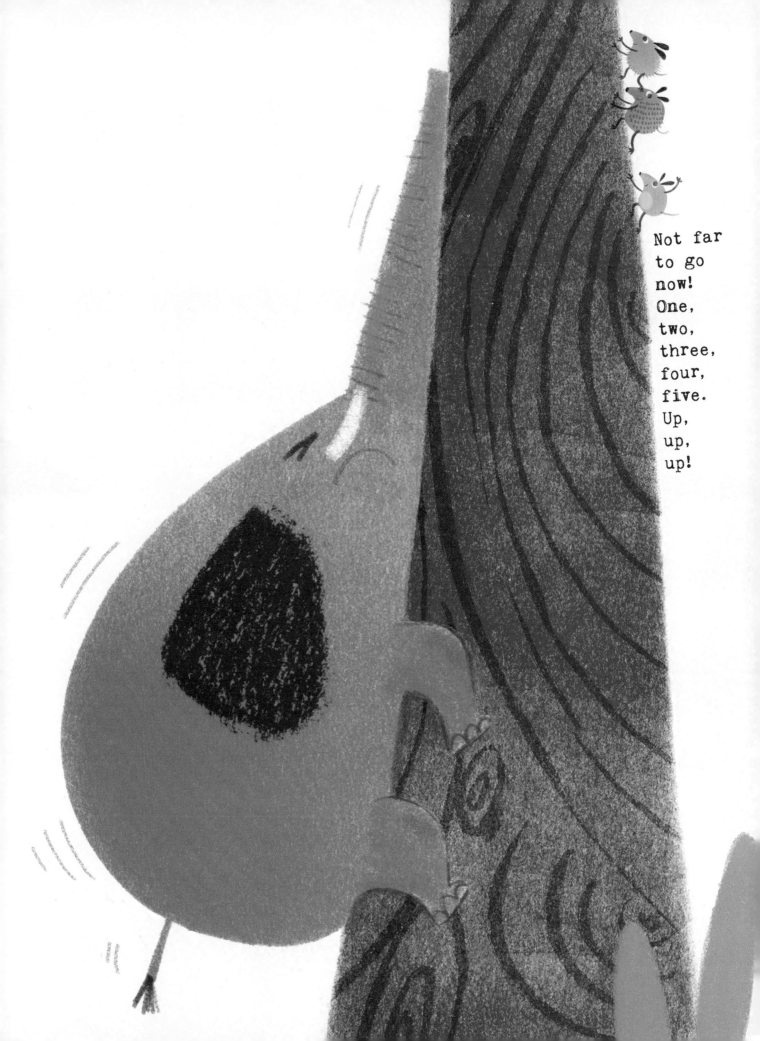

Not far
to go
now!
One,
two,
three,
four,
five.
Up,
up,
up!

OOF!

He didn't get very far at all.

I can almost reeeeeeach!

The elephants were getting VERY impatient
and VERY hungry! Elephant Four decided
to just run at the tree as fast as he could.

"MINE!"

"MINE!"

said the elephants, all at once.
But just at that moment ...

the delicious-looking exotic fruit began ...

Now the delicious-looking exotic fruit belonged
to the five mice, who carried it ... TOGETHER!
"This fruit is OURS!" the five mice said.

The elephants looked on, astonished.

"OURS?"

said the elephants.

Hooray!
We've got
the fruit!

"OURS!"

said the elephants, all at once.

"Why didn't *we* think of that!?"

Huff!

Puff!

"OURS!"

Huff!

He-e-e-e-a-v-e!

"OURS!"
Stre-e-e-etch!

"This fruit is OURS!"

And that's how, deep, *deep* in the heart of the jungle, the elephants finally got their delicious-looking exotic fruit.

"Weren't there five of us?"

"OURS!"

Thank you most of all to Mum and my brother Alberto.

Thank you to Martin Salisbury, Alexis Deacon, Anne-Louise Jones, Maria Tunney and Helen Mackenzie-Smith.

Thank you all for making it possible for me to create this book, my first picture book!

First published 2018 by Walker Books Ltd, 87 Vauxhall Walk, London SE11 5HJ • This edition published 2019 • © 2018 Anuska Allepuz
The right of Anuska Allepuz to be identified as author/illustrator of this work has been asserted by her in accordance with the Copyright, Designs and Patents Act 1988 • This book has been typeset in Didact Gothic • Printed in China • All rights reserved. No part of this book may be reproduced, transmitted or stored in an information retrieval system in any form or by any means, graphic, electronic or mechanical, including photocopying, taping and recording, without prior written permission from the publisher. British Library Cataloguing in Publication Data: a catalogue record for this book is available from the British Library
ISBN 978-1-4063-8286-0 • www.walker.co.uk • 10 9 8 7 6 5 4 3 2 1